WHERE'S THE
STRIKER?

EGMONT

We bring stories to life

First published in Great Britain in 2020 by Egmont Books UK Ltd
2 Minster Court, 10th floor, London EC3R 7BB.
www.egmontbooks.co.uk

Written by Craig Jelley
Designed by Richie Hull
Illustrations by Paul Moran and Gergely Forizs
(Pages 8-15, 18-21, 24-27, 30-35 and 38)
Illustrations by Daniel Limon
(Pages 16-17, 22-23, 28-29)
This book is an original creation by Egmont Books UK Ltd.

ISBN 978 1 4052 9701 1
70872/001
Printed in Italy

WHERE'S THE

STRIKER?

★ ★ MEET THE ★ ★ ALL-STARS

Assembled for the upcoming Continental Championship, the All-Stars XI features the best players from around the globe, handpicked by manager Terry Gafferson. Hopes are high that this team can become true world-beaters.

WORLDIE

TERRY GAFFERSON

DAVID DE GEA

KALIDOU KOULIBAILY

VIRGIL VAN DIJK

MARCELO

LUCY BRONZE

EDEN HAZARD

HEUNG-MIN SON

PAUL POGBA

ADA HEGERBERG

LIONEL MESSI

HARRY KANE

Find out how the All-Stars fare on their campaign across the continents and see if you can spot every player in each location. Give yourself a bonus point for spotting Worldie, the team's mascot in every scene too.

CONTENTS

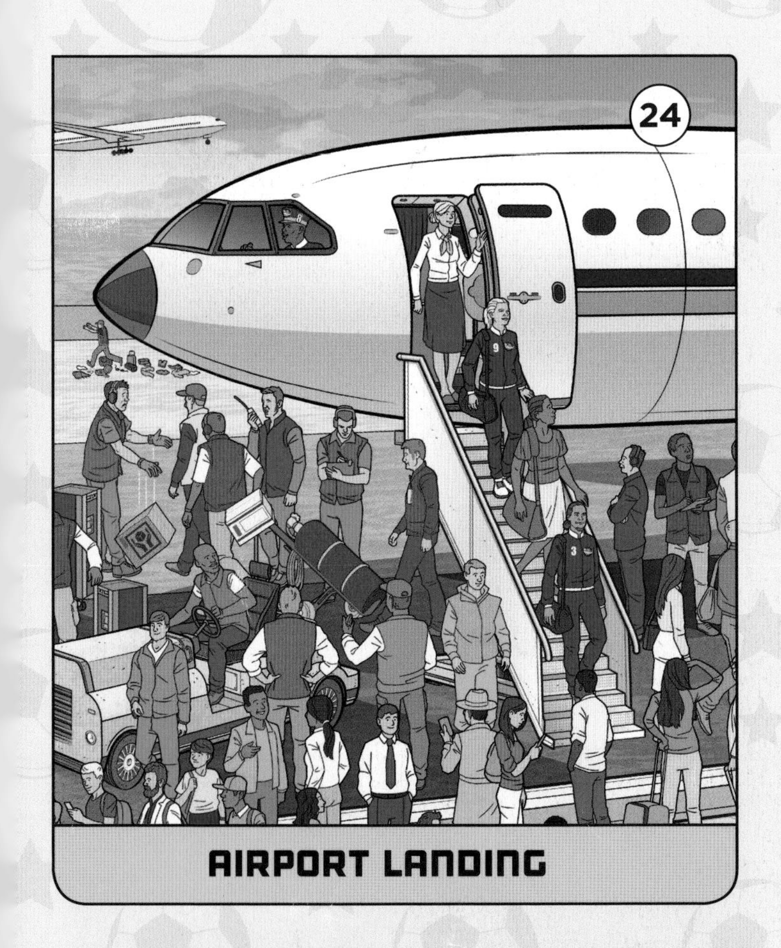

AIRPORT LANDING

PENALTY SHOOTOUT

STRANGEST HAIRCUTS

TUNNEL NERVES

THEY THINK IT'S ALL OVER

VICTORY PARADE

MORE TO FIND

HEROES' WELCOME
The All-Stars arrive at their home stadium for the first game of the Continental Championship. Hundreds of excited fans have arrived at the ground to welcome them. The team have no choice but to meet and greet them as they wade their way towards the entrance.
3
4

OPENING MATCH

The All-Stars are facing the fearsome African Lions in the first round of the tournament. Their opponents are tough, but they eventually get an opportunity to score from a looping corner. Harry Kane smashes a bicycle kick right into the top corner!

3 A.M.
3 A.M.
HOTEL HIJINKS
After defeating the African Lions in the first round, the team head to their hotel to relax and blow off some steam before they travel to their next match. With the manager fast asleep, the team begin to get up to mischief in the hotel lobby.

WARMING UP
With a few hours' sleep under their belts, the All-Stars are back at the stadium for their second game against the Eastern Dragons, who are raring to go! There are just minutes before the teams go head-to-head, perfect for running some last-minute drills and warm-ups.

CELEBRATE LIKE A PRO

STJARNAN FC
CATCH OF THE DAY
CAST YOUR ROD AND REEL IN A TEAMMATE
Enlist your pals to lift the catch
Pose for a photo
TIM CAHILL
FLAG KNOCKOUT
GLOAT WITH TEAMMATES
Approach innocent corner flag
Left, right, left, right, hook
ROBBIE KEANE
ROLLING THUNDER
Finger-guns: Pyew-pyew!
Fall into a forward-roll
Launch into a cartwheel
JIMMY BULLARD
ANGRY MANAGER
HOPE THE BOSS STILL PICKS YOU FOR THE NEXT MATCH
Wag your finger at teammates disapprovingly
Sit the team down in a circle
ALAN SHEARER
SIMPLE SALUTE
LOW-ENERGY, PERFECT FOR REPEATED USE
Raise a single hand
Race off in jubilation

BEACH BONDING
The All-Stars narrowly squeezed past the Dragons in the last round, but the manager thinks they can do better. He's taken them on a team bonding trip to try and improve the squad chemistry before the semi-final.

THE GOLDEN BALL
The Continental Championship is the last tournament of a busy season and players from across the world have gathered at a fancy awards show, The Golden Ball, to recognise the greatest players of the year. Can you spot the All-Stars in their smart attire?
POPCORN

THE MODERN PROFESSIONAL

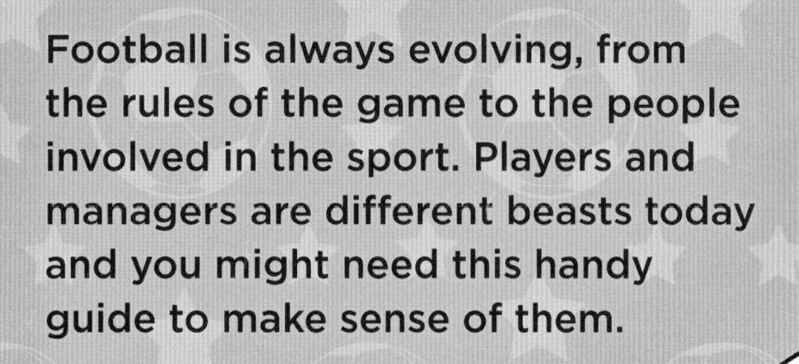

Football is always evolving, from the rules of the game to the people involved in the sport. Players and managers are different beasts today and you might need this handy guide to make sense of them.

HAIRCUT

The most important aspect of any modern player.

Changes more often than the shirt.

SHIRT

Detachable at the expense of a yellow card.

Replicas cost a small fortune.

Generally untucked.

CLUB BADGE

Insignia worn with pride by fans and locals.

Reminds pros who they're playing for this season.

TATTOO

Blank skin is wasted space.

Normally ties in to the player 'brand'.

BOTTLE

Contains invigorating isotonic swill.

Many pros lose it in the biggest games.

ARMS

Evolutionarily intended for balance.

Footballers flail around wildly while falling.

SQUAD NUMBER

Once a sign of importance in squad; the lower the better.

Now largely random and has no relation to player quality.

BOOTS

Featherweight to maximise speed (and ankle injuries).

Gaudy colours. No longer possible to find plain black boots.

THE MODERN MANAGER

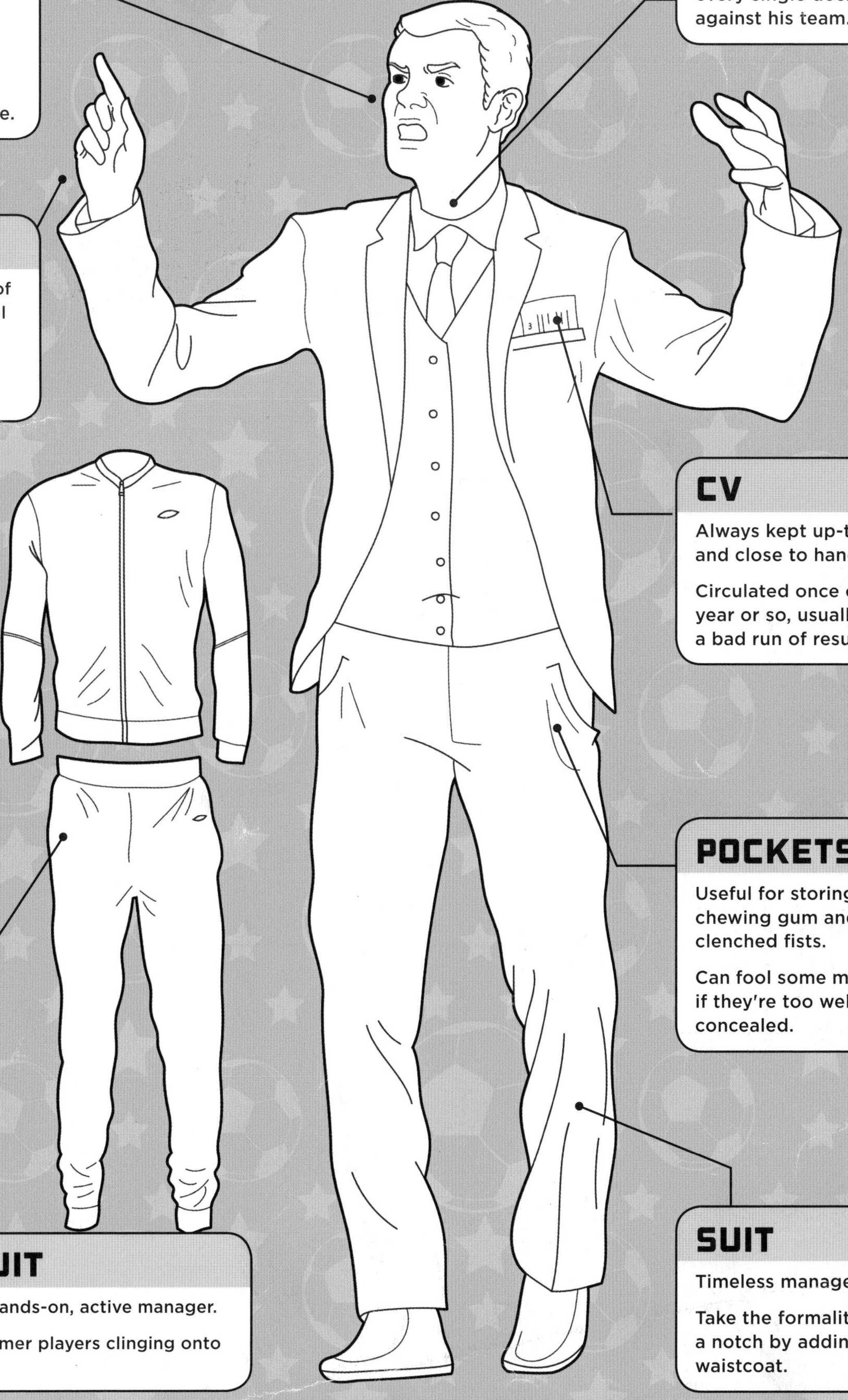

SCOWL

Default expression for watching a match.

Also useful for scaring journalists in the post-match press conference.

THROAT

Hoarse from contesting every single decision against his team.

HANDS

Contort to a multitude of supposedly instructional gestures.

Baffle opposition and own team alike.

CV

Always kept up-to-date and close to hand.

Circulated once every year or so, usually after a bad run of results.

POCKETS

Useful for storing pens, chewing gum and clenched fists.

Can fool some managers if they're too well-concealed.

TRACKSUIT

Signifies a more hands-on, active manager.

Often worn by former players clinging onto their youth.

SUIT

Timeless manager look.

Take the formality down a notch by adding in a waistcoat.

AIRPORT LANDING

The semi-final is an away game for the All-Stars, so they've jetted across the Atlantic for the next match. The players are keen to head straight to the game, but first they've got to make it through border control!

1
2
4

PENALTY SHOOTOUT

After a nail-biting 90 minutes, and a tense period of extra-time, the American Wildcats have held the All-Stars to a draw and taken the game to a sudden-death penalty shootout. If the All-Stars can hold their nerve and slot this final spot-kick away, they're in the final!

STRANGEST HAIRCUTS

With the amount of money flowing through football, you'd expect footballers to be able to afford a decent haircut – unfortunately, that doesn't always seem to be the case. Here are the most unusual trims ever to grace the football pitch.

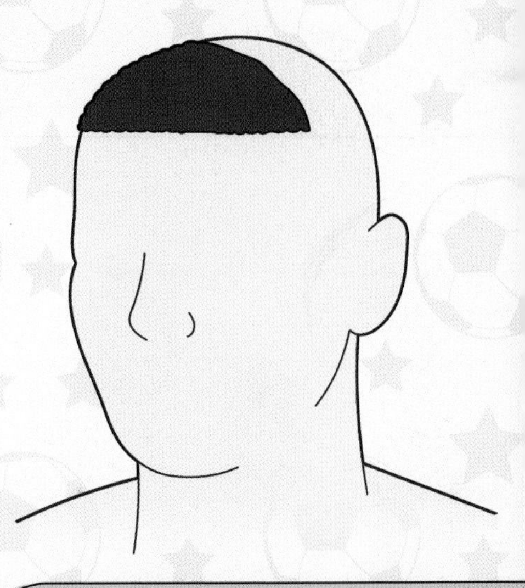

'THE HALF MOON'
RONALDO

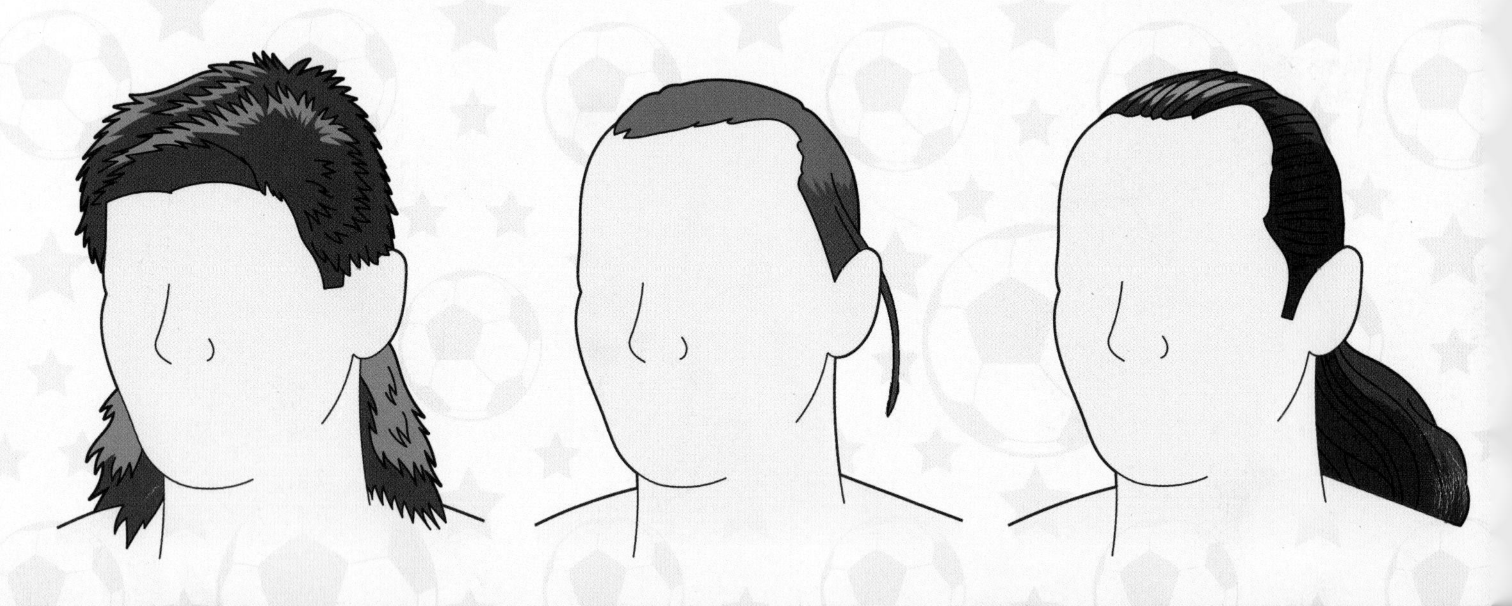

'THE MULLET'
CHRIS WADDLE

'THE RAT TAIL'
RODRIGO PALACIO

'THE PONY'
DAVID SEAMAN

'THE COMBOVER'
BOBBY CHARLTON

'THE CURTAINS'
GERVINHO

'THE BLONDE MANE'
CARLOS VALDERRAMA

'IL DIVIN CODINO'
ROBERTO BAGGIO

'THE FAUX-HAWK'
DAVID BECKHAM

'THE FRIAR'
GIOVANNI SIMEONE

'THE SIDESHOW BOB'
DAVID LUIZ

'THE PATRIOT'
TARIBO WEST

'THE SPIDER'
MANUEL CANGE

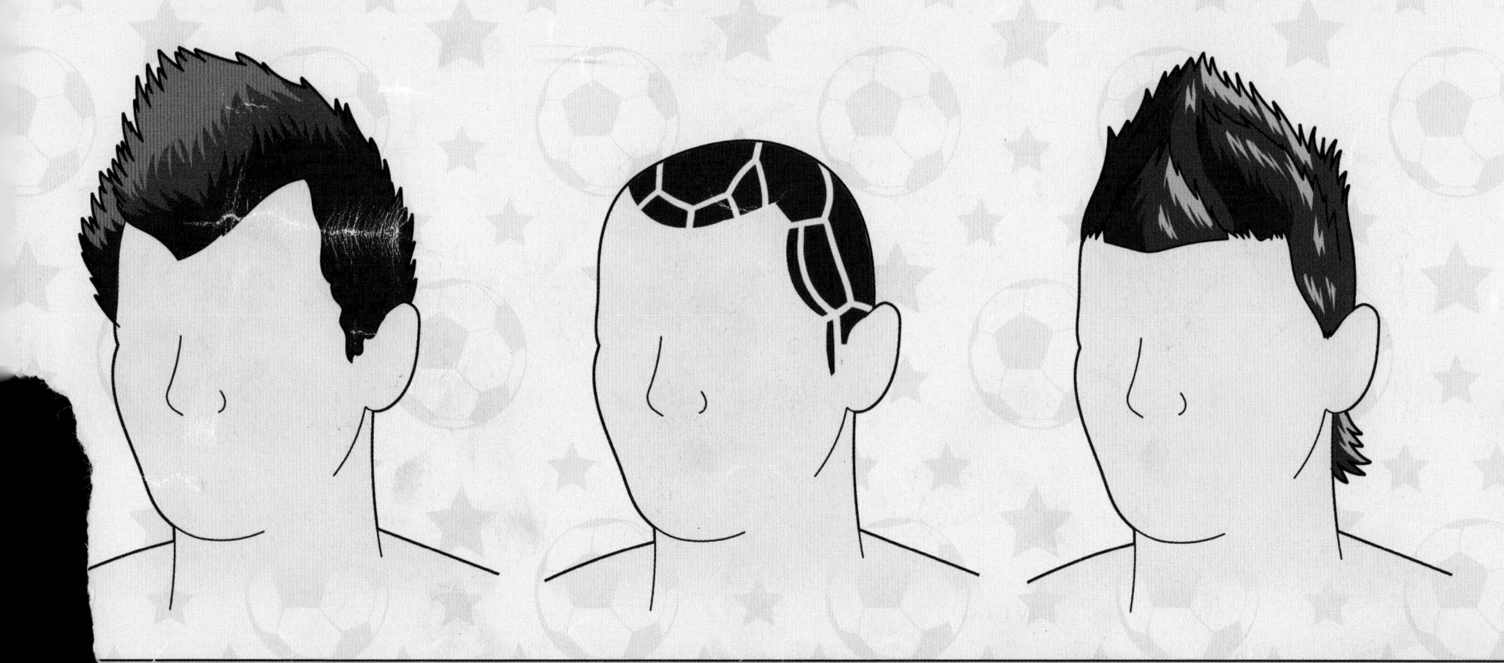

'THE NEON'
REDDIE LJUNGBERG

'THE HEADER'
RATINHO

'THE GEL MOUNTAIN'
MAROUANE CHAMAKH

TUNNEL NERVES
All roads have led to this moment – the Continental Championship final. The two finalists – the All-Stars and the Euro Titans – nervously make their way down the tunnel as legions of adoring fans cheer them on. It's a tense wait for all before the game kicks off!

THEY THINK IT'S ALL OVER
Both teams battled bravely and gave every last ounce of energy over 90 minutes. At the end of a hard-fought match, the All-Stars scored a late winner! They've won the cup! The fans go wild and invade the pitch to celebrate with the team as the Euro Titans trudge off.

UICTORY PARADE
The All-Stars put on a parade to show off their shiny new trophy and fans travel in droves to see their world-beating heroes. They've defeated every team that stood in their way and now they're looking forward to defending their crown at the next tournament.

MORE TO FIND

Your globetrotting journey with the All-Stars has ended, but there's plenty to still to discover. See if you can find all these items on each page.

HEROES' WELCOME

- [ ] An autograph hunter
- [ ] A programme seller
- [ ] A bicycle kick
- [ ] A football-patterned blimp
- [ ] A witch's cauldron

OPENING MATCH

- [ ] The captain's armband
- [ ] Top bin
- [ ] A super sub
- [ ] A fan blowing a vuvuzela
- [ ] A midfield general

HOTEL HIJINKS

- [ ] Early doors
- [ ] A player receiving the hairdryer treatment
- [ ] Teammates playing a football video game
- [ ] Clean sheet

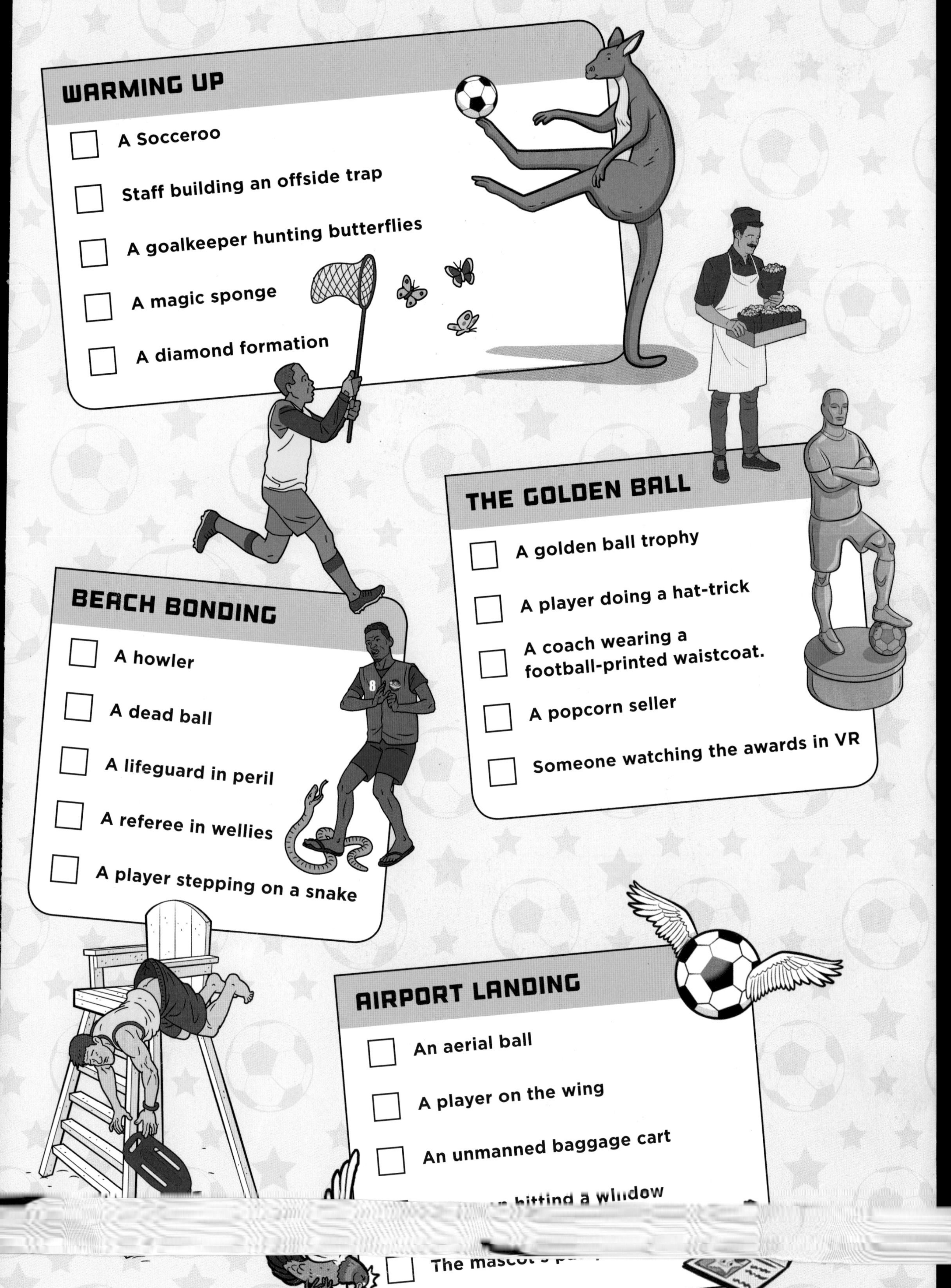
WARMING UP
A Socceroo
Staff building an offside trap
A goalkeeper hunting butterflies
A magic sponge
A diamond formation
THE GOLDEN BALL
A golden ball trophy
A player doing a hat-trick
A coach wearing a football-printed waistcoat.
A popcorn seller
Someone watching the awards in VR
BEACH BONDING
A howler
A dead ball
A lifeguard in peril
A referee in wellies
A player stepping on a snake
AIRPORT LANDING
An aerial ball
A player on the wing
An unmanned baggage cart
hitting a window
8

PENALTY SHOOTOUT
A Mexican wave
A player taking an early bath
A fox in a box
A footballing postman
A hand-printed ball
TUNNEL NERVES
Someone vacuuming the carpet
A trophy thief
A lady knitting a trophy
A malfunctioning security drone
THEY THINK IT'S ALL OVER
The 'Poznan'
An All-Stars player doing an interview
A dog digging up a trophy
A Titans-themed wardrobe
VICTORY PARADE
A crash-test dummy
A trophy-shaped balloon
The Continental Championship trophy
A dribbling cow
A fan holding a flare

The All-Stars aren't the only legends hiding in this book. Can you find the players below somewhere along the adventure? There may be some surprise stars hidden in scenes too!

AMERICAN WILDCATS

AFRICAN LIONS

EASTERN DRAGONS

EURO TITANS

FOOTBALL GLOSSARY

Sometimes football folk around the world use silly phrases for simple things that happen on and around the pitch. Here's a cheat sheet so you know what they're talking about.

Aerial Ball – a lofted ball that travels through the air.

Bicycle Kick (UK) – an acrobatic kick that looks like you're riding a bike upside down.

Butterfly Hunter (Hungary) – a keeper who leaps for a cross, flapping his hands and misses the ball.

Captain's Armband – a band that a team's captain wears to show he's in charge.

Clean Sheet (UK) – when a team doesn't concede a goal

Cow Dribble (Portugal) – knocking the ball one side of a defender, then running round the other side to meet it.

Dead Ball (UK) – a free-kick or penalty, so called because the ball must be still, or 'dead' before it is taken.

Diamond Formation – a midfield that involves one midfield ahead of two central midfielders, while another plays behind, making a diamond shape.

Dummy (UK) – a faking move to trick an opposing player.

Early Bath (UK) – when a player is sent off, they're said to be going for an early bath.

Early Doors (UK) – the first few minutes of a football match.

Elevator Team (Germany) – a domestic team that gets relegated one season and promoted the next (or vice versa).

Fox in the Box – a term for a striker that hangs around the opposition area, looking to pop up when the ball comes their way and poke it in the net.

Hairdryer Treatment (UK) – a telling-off from the manager.

Handball – purposely playing the ball with one's hand.

Hat Trick – when a player scores three goals in a match.

Howler (UK) – a terrible mistake or a bad attempt on goal.

Knitting (France) – when a player strings together lots of unnecessary skills.

Magic Sponge (UK) – a simple wet sponge that seems to heal all ailments that afflict footballers.

Mexican Wave – a crowd-based action that involves standing up and sitting down in sequence to simulate a wave travelling around the stadium.

Midfield General – a commanding midfielder who controls the flow of a match.

Offside Trap – a tactic that involves defenders stepping up quickly so that opposition strikers are in an offside position.

Pigeon's Wing (France) – flicking an aerial ball on by [illegible]